I'd never been to Chicago before. I hadn't even ridden a train.

Mom went over the instructions with me about fifty times. She was going to drive me to the commuter station where we'd buy my ticket. It was to be a round trip. I'd use half on the way in and half on the way back. She'd watch while I got on the train and found a seat. I was to stay in that seat until the train pulled into Chicago. I wasn't supposed to talk to strangers. My aunt would be waiting for me when I got off the train.

It sounded simple enough. I couldn't figure out why my mom was getting so bent out of shape.

A JOSH McINTIRE BOOK

OPERATION GARBAGE

Elaine K. McEwan

Chariot Books™
David C. Cook Publishing Co.

Published by Chariot Books™,
an imprint of David C. Cook Publishing Co.
David C. Cook Publishing Co., Elgin, Illinois 60120
David C. Cook Publishing Co., Weston, Ontario
Nova Distribution Ltd., Eastbourne, England

OPERATION GARBAGE
© 1993 by Elaine K. McEwan

McGee and Me!, McGee character and McGee and Me!
logo are registered trademarks of Tyndale House
Publishers, Inc. Used by permission.

Cover illustration by Robert Papp
Cover design by Elizabeth Thompson
First printing, 1993
Printed in the United States of America
97 96 95 94   5 4 3 2

Library of Congress Cataloging-in-Publication Data
McEwan, Elaine K.
Operation Garbage: a Josh McIntire book/Elaine K. McEwan.
        p.   cm.
"Chariot Books."
Summary: The success of his class project on hazardous wastes
and his involvement with a group of Christian friends helps
fifth-grader Josh McIntire deal with his feelings since his
parents' divorce.
ISBN 0-7814-0121-6
[1. Refuse and refuse disposal—Fiction. 2. Hazardous
wastes—Fiction. 3. Schools—Fiction. 4. Divorce—Fiction 5.
Christian life—Fiction] I. Title
PZ7.M159250p
[Fic]—dc20   92-43761
                                                        CIP
                                                        AC

To Ray
still a little boy at heart

I didn't want to go back to school. Two weeks of Christmas vacation weren't enough. I'd put together the models my dad sent me, and Wendell and I had built a really neat snow fort in the backyard. Just the thought of doing homework again was making me feel sick.

I looked at my face in the bathroom mirror for spots. No such luck. It was probably just a case of "back-to-school-itis."

"Joshua!" yelled Mom. "I need to put on my makeup. What are you doing in there?"

Her voice startled me out of my daydreaming. Well, maybe school wouldn't be that bad after all. I'd see Tracy and Trevor again. And Mrs. Bannister had mentioned something about garbage being our project for the new year. Looking in my desk had probably given her the idea. I hadn't cleaned it out since Open House, and I could hardly put the top down.

I splashed some water on my face and ran a comb

through my hair. I wondered if Tracy would notice my new Chicago Bears shirt. It had the team logo in orange and blue on the front. I smoothed my hair just a little bit more and wondered for the hundredth time if I should get a spiked haircut.

Mom rapped sharply on the door and called once more in an impatient tone. "Are you on another planet this morning? Or did you fall in?"

"Aw, Mom," I groaned. She made bad jokes like that all the time and expected me to laugh at them.

"I'm sorry," I said as I stepped aside in the doorway to let her in. "I don't feel like going to school."

"That's natural," she said. "But all play and no work makes Jack a dull boy."

"My name is Joshua. Besides, I thought it was all work and no play that made Jack dull."

"The principle's the same," she stated firmly. My mom loves quotations and sayings.

I leaned against the door and watched her. Why do girls draw lines on their eyebrows and paint stuff on their lips? I'm glad I'm not a girl.

"Josh," she said softly, as she patted her face with powder. "I've got something to tell you."

I could tell this was important.

She wasn't looking at me. "I got a call from someone you know this week," she said.

My stomach stopped aching and did flip-flops. It had to be Dad. My mom and dad were divorced. But ever since I'd become a Christian, I'd been praying they'd get back together again. Maybe this was my answer.

"What did he want?" I asked.

"That someone wasn't Dad," she answered.

"I don't get it," I said. "You said it was someone I knew. Who else would call you?"

"Sonny Studebaker," she said.

"What did he want?"

"He wanted to take me out on a date," she said.

All of a sudden I felt strange, and I must have looked that way too.

"I know this is hard for you, Joshua," she began.

"You can't go out on dates," I said. "You're my mom!" My voice got louder. "And especially not with Sonny. He's *my* friend."

By the time I'd reached the end of my speech, I was shouting hysterically. I ran to my bedroom, slammed the door, and turned the lock into place. Mom had sure picked a great time to lay this one on me.

She knocked on the door several times, but I didn't answer.

"Josh, I didn't say I was going out with him," she said. "I just wanted you to know he asked me."

"Go away," I said. "I don't want to talk to you."

"I have to go to work," she said. "Please come out."

"Just leave me alone," I sobbed." I hated to cry,

even though Sonny says it's good for you. But suddenly I wasn't sure I could trust Sonny anymore.

"Josh, I can't be late for work," she pleaded. "Please come out before I leave."

I turned the lock and slowly opened the bedroom door. Mom's face was tear-stained too. The makeup she had just put on was smeared and running.

"We'll talk about it tonight," she said. "I should have realized how upset you'd be. I'm sorry." She gave me a quick hug and ran to the front door.

And I'd thought all I had to worry about was going back to school.

The phone interrupted my thoughts.

"Hi. Are you ready?" It was Wendell.

Wendell is my next-door neighbor. He's in my class at school, and I've learned a lot of stuff from him. But sometimes he acts more like a grown-up than some grown-ups I know.

I cleared my throat and tried to sound normal. "Sure, I'll meet you out front."

I splashed water over my face for a second time that morning, grabbed my jacket and book bag, and walked slowly down the front steps.

It was cold and sunny. Snow had fallen during the night, and everything looked white and fresh. If my mom had remembered, she'd have made me wear boots. Of course, nobody but little kids wear boots to school, but moms always make you buy them.

Even Wendell, the kid with no fashion sense, doesn't wear boots.

"What do you think this garbage project will be about?" asked Wendell.

I wasn't in the mood for talking about school, but I didn't want to talk about my problems either.

"I dunno," I muttered.

Wendell didn't seem to notice my reluctance. He chattered nonstop as we slid along the sidewalks to Jefferson School.

Everyone was huddled in little groups on the playground. It was as if we needed to get reacquainted after the vacation. Either that or we were all too frozen to play our usual games of dodgeball and tag. But the fresh air made me feel better. Mom hadn't said she'd go out with Sonny, just that he'd asked her. But why would he do a thing like that?

When the bell rang we lined up as usual. I spotted Tracy Kendall and smiled at her. She gave me a little wave. She looked different, and at first I couldn't figure out what it was. Then it dawned on me. She was wearing glasses. Why'd she have to go and spoil her looks with glasses?

At least I could depend on Wendell to be predictable. He was wearing the same ugly green plaid shirt and polyester pants he'd worn the first day we met. . . .

Mrs. Bannister had changed over vacation too. She'd cut off her springy gray curls and was sporting a new hairdo. She looked less like my grandmother now. But she still had her whistle, glasses, and several pens jangling on assorted chains around her neck.

"Your hair looks nice, Mrs. Bannister," gushed Samantha Sullivan. She was always looking for a chance to impress the teacher. But Mrs. Bannister looked embarrassed and got right down to business.

"Good morning, everyone," she said briskly. "I hope you've made some New Year's resolutions to work harder this year."

Inwardly I groaned. My first report card in November wasn't too bad. I'd done a great report on cockroaches for science and a pretty good one on the Underground Railroad for social studies. My big problem was keeping track of the daily homework Mrs. Bannister assigned. I kept losing papers in my desk. And sometimes I couldn't concentrate. I'd think about my parents getting back together again or moving back to my old house in Woodview. Or I'd just make up stuff inside my head. But I had to admit that Mrs. Bannister was the most interesting teacher I'd ever had. She let us do messy things in class and work in groups.

"We're going to be starting Operation Garbage today," Mrs. Bannister announced. This sounded like it could easily be the messiest thing we'd done yet.

"What's Operation Garbage?" Trevor whispered in my ear. Trevor has Down's syndrome and is in my group. He has a hard time learning some of the stuff we do in class and he asks me a lot of questions. But Mrs. Bannister never minds if I'm talking to Trevor. She knows I'm helping him.

"I haven't got a clue," I answered. "Sh-h." I put my finger across my lips. Sometimes Trevor doesn't catch on that he's supposed to be quiet while Mrs. Bannister is talking.

"Garbage is a real problem in our world today," Mrs. Bannister went on. "And here in 5B we're going to do something about it."

I couldn't imagine what twenty-six fifth graders could do about the garbage problem in the world except take it out more often. It wasn't one of my favorite jobs. The coffee grounds always seemed to be leaking through the bag, and once the whole bottom fell out and covered my feet in potato peelings and leftover Jell-O. It was not a pretty sight. And then there was the matter of taking the cans down to the curb every Monday night and bringing them back to the garage every Tuesday afternoon. There was enough garbage in my life at home. I didn't need any more at school.

Mrs. Bannister went on, oblivious to my distaste for the subject. "What comes to your mind when I talk about a garbage problem?" she asked.

I decided to be brave and raise my hand.

"Josh?" she said.

"Well, it smells," I ventured, wrinkling my nose in disgust.

Everybody laughed. Even Mrs. Bannister.

"That is a problem," she said. "We all throw away many pounds of garbage every day, and it doesn't just disappear. And if you have lots of garbage decomposing, you have some very unpleasant odors."

I gave myself a silent cheer for coming up with a good answer.

"What other problems can you think of?" she continued.

Tracy raised her hand. Our group was really coming through this morning. "We're running out of places to put all of our garbage," she said.

"Excellent," said Mrs. Bannister.

I smiled over at Tracy. Maybe her glasses didn't

look that bad. They matched her red hair.

"That's the whole point of what I'm talking about," Mrs. Bannister went on. "We need to figure out ways to reduce, reuse, and recycle. By the end of this project, I don't want you throwing anything away without first thinking about reducing, reusing, and recycling."

"I thought reducing was something you did to fractions," said Ben.

Mrs. Bannister chuckled at Ben's little joke. She sure was in a good mood.

"During the next few weeks, 5B is going to work on reducing the amount of garbage in our world," she explained. "If we can do it here at Jefferson School, then maybe we can help the whole world."

I envisioned Mrs. Bannister supervising a fleet of garbage trucks, each driven by a Jefferson School fifth grader, cruising all around the world picking up trash. She'd be wearing coveralls, big rubber boots, and a safari hat. But she'd still have her glasses and whistle and pens.

"Joshua."

I heard my name being called but I didn't know why. My face turned red. I had to stop daydreaming and pay attention.

Trevor whispered in my ear. "Mrs. Bannister wants to know if you'll be in charge of our group."

Thank goodness for Trevor. He'd been listening.

16

I nodded in response to Mrs. Bannister's request.

"This is a big responsibility, Joshua," she explained, "but I'm sure you'll be up to it."

Did I have a choice?

She went on to assign other team captains, and Project Garbage was launched. Our mission, she said, was to reduce the amount of garbage at Jefferson School. Mrs. Bannister gave our groups a chance to talk to each other and write down all of the ideas we could think of. She called it brainstorming.

I had already thought of a great way to reduce garbage at lunch time: serve decent food. Monday was pizza day and that was okay. But sometimes they served the most disgusting ham patty sandwiches with "ear wax." That's what we call the sweet potatoes that come with the ham. If the cafeteria served McDonald's hamburgers, we'd reduce garbage. I was already thinking of how to persuade Mrs. Raymond, the principal.

Tracy was writing our ideas down. She listed mine first, and I felt terrific. The feeling lasted until, out of nowhere, I remembered what Mom had told me that morning. I still couldn't believe it. Sonny was my friend.

The group had come up with more good ideas while I was daydreaming. Tracy wanted to put a big garbage can in our room so people could bring their empty pop cans to school.

"We can take them to the recycling center," she explained.

Trevor said we should write on both sides of our notebook paper.

And Sarah came up with the best suggestion of all. "We can have a garage sale to sell all the things we don't want instead of throwing them away," she explained.

I liked the feeling of being in a group. Somehow it made schoolwork less scary if I could check it out with somebody else.

"That's all on Operation Garbage for today, class," said Mrs. Bannister. "We have to move on. Tomorrow we'll talk about our ideas and decide which ones we'll do. We'll also talk about writing reports."

Just then a blond woman I'd never seen before stuck her head in the door. She motioned to one of the students who got up and left.

"Who was that?" I asked Tracy.

"Oh, that's Mrs. Ellison, the social worker," she said.

"What's a social worker?" I asked.

"She talks to you if your parents are getting a divorce and helps you adjust to it," she explained.

I'd never heard of a social worker before. What a weird name. It sounded like somebody who should plan parties, not help kids whose parents were splitting up. Did she talk to kids even after their parents were divorced, or just while it was happening,

I wondered. And did she cost money like the dentist? Mom said I had to wait to have my teeth cleaned until her insurance coverage was better.

Life was sure complicated. Maybe I'd ask the secretary, Mrs. Turner. She seemed to know the answers to everything. Once when I forgot my lunch money, she loaned me a dollar.

After school, I hung around the office until Mrs. Turner was alone.

"Hi, Josh," she greeted me. "Forget your lunch money again?"

I smiled. "Nah," I answered. Now that I had come, I didn't have the courage to ask my question.

"So, what can I do for you? Or is this just a social call?"

At the mention of the word social, my face turned red. Did she already know why I was there? Did everybody know my parents were divorced?

"Are you sick?" she asked. Now her questions were becoming more persistent. "Do I need to call your mother?"

"I need to know about social workers," I said.

"What do you need to know?" she asked.

"Well, do you have to pay for them?" I asked.

"They don't work for nothing," she replied.

"That's not what I meant," I explained. "If somebody at school wants to see the social worker, do they have to pay her?"

Mrs. Turner laughed. "Of course not, Joshua. Working with students is part of her job. That's what she gets a salary for. You don't need a social worker, do you?"

I was embarrassed. "Nah, not really," I replied. "See you later."

I turned and left the office. Now I'd lost my chance.

I didn't want to go home, but I didn't have anywhere else to go. Normally I would have stopped in to see Sonny. I hadn't worked during Christmas vacation, and I missed our conversations. But I couldn't face him yet.

The wind was cold, and the sky was dark and stormy. Just like my mood. Light flakes of snow brushed my cheeks as I walked toward home. They mixed with my tears. I couldn't believe it. Twice in the same day.

I knew what I needed to do . . . pray.

Dear God, I began, *I'm in another jam and I don't know what to do. Why can't I figure things out like Wendell? He never seems to have any problems, but nothing goes right for me. Do You love Wendell more than me? I don't even know what I want. I thought my big problem was Mom and Dad being divorced, but now I'm not sure. It looks like my big problem is Mom and Sonny. What is my problem anyway, God?*

Mom's car was in the driveway. She must have

left work early. I could smell dinner cooking the minute I opened the front door. The faint fragrance of her perfume mixed with the aroma of pot roast. She came into the living room and ran to give me a big hug.

"Oh, Josh, I'm so glad to see you. You're late. I was worried that something had happened to you." The words tumbled out pell-mell.

"I just stayed a few minutes to talk to the secretary," I explained.

"Why?" she asked.

This was the time to go for it. If I didn't say something now, I might not get another chance.

"I wanted to ask about the school social worker," I said. "She sees kids whose parents are divorced."

Mom's face brightened. "I think that's a great idea," she said. "I didn't know you could do that."

I suddenly felt much better. Maybe Mom did understand.

"Dinner's ready. You'll have to leave for your karate lesson soon, so get washed up," she urged.

I didn't need a second invitation. She'd fixed roasted potatoes, creamed corn, muffins, and a fruit salad. This was like the old days when Dad was around.

"Let's pray before we eat," Mom suggested.

I was surprised, but I bowed my head, and she spoke aloud. "Dear Father, I thank You for my son

21

Joshua and how much he means to me. Watch over him and care for him. Keep him close to You, God. I know You love him as much as I do. Help us to work out our problems together. Bless this food. In Your name. Amen."

I stared at her in amazement. "I didn't know you could pray, Mom," I said.

"There are lots of things you don't know about me, Joshua," she said. "I used to be the leader of my church youth group when I was in high school."

"How come I've never heard you pray before?" I asked.

She looked uncomfortable. "Lots of reasons, but we don't have time to discuss them right now. You need to eat your dinner and get into your *gi* for karate."

I could tell when to stop asking questions.

I was all fired up about garbage. I couldn't wait to tell Mom about my idea for a report. Mrs. Bannister had explained that along with our group projects, we each had to write our own report. She said we had to be accountable both as a group and as individuals. Accountability was her new word for the year. It meant you had to do what you were supposed to do.

I decided it was going to be my word for the year too. Along with my year verse. My Awana leader, Mr. Barron, said we each had to choose a Bible verse that would be ours for the new year. The verse was supposed to help us whenever we had a problem. And mine had to do with accountability. I hadn't been too accountable during the past year, and I'd decided that things had to change.

While I ate my peanut butter toast snack, I thought about my verse. "I will try to walk a blame-less path, but how I need your help, especially in my own home, where I long to act as I should" (Psalm 101:2). I'd memorized it during vacation. Mr. Barron helped me find it when I told him I wanted to do a better job of making the right decisions about things. He said that God would be there to help me, but I'd have to do my part too.

Tonight was Awana, and I was anxious to tell Mr. Barron about the good decision I'd made yesterday to go right home from school, instead of running off someplace because I was mad.

I heard Mom's car and put my dirty dishes in the sink.

"Hi, Mom!" I shouted as she came through the door. "I've got to tell you about my garbage project. Where's a big library I can go to?"

"Whoa. Wait a minute," she said. "Let me get my coat off and have a cup of tea first."

"Okay," I said. "But I want to do the best report I've ever done, and if I go to a big library I can find things that no one else will be able to find."

She put some water on to boil and dropped a tea bag in her favorite mug. It said, "Make Tea, Not War." I didn't get it, but I'd never asked her what it meant.

"So tell me about this report," she said. "Is this going to get you in trouble again like your last two reports?"

"Oh, no, Mom," I asserted. "I'm going to be accountable this year."

She smiled broadly. "What does that mean?"

I explained about Mrs. Bannister and Mr. Barron and how they were both into accountability. "I'm not sure that Mrs. Bannister knows about God wanting us to be accountable," I said. "But it can't hurt to have both of them checking up on me.

"So," I went on, "I need to go to a big library and do my research."

Mom thought for a moment. "I know," she said. "Aunt Kathy's university has a big library. Would that do?"

"Yeah, that would be cool," I said. My aunt is a professor of anthropology—whatever that is—in Chicago. "When can we call her?"

"We'd better get some dinner made first," she cautioned. "You have Awana tonight. I'll call her and make the arrangements while you're there."

I finished my math at the kitchen table while she stir-fried some chicken and vegetables. Was it my imagination, or was my mother getting to be a better cook all of a sudden?

Wendell picked me up, and we walked the short distance to the Grandville Community Church. Awana was held in the gym.

Tracy Kendall arrived just as we did. She gave me a cheerful wave and a hello. Somehow I got tongue-tied and shy whenever Tracy was around. And Wendell wasn't any help at all. He was already on the other side of the gym talking to Mr. Barron, our leader.

Tracy didn't seem to notice my awkwardness.

"What are you going to do your report on?" she asked.

"I'm not sure," I answered. "Maybe toxic waste. But I'm gonna go to Chicago to do my research."

I could tell Tracy was impressed.

"Wow," she said. "That's really neat."

I wanted to keep the conversation going, but I couldn't think of anything else to say.

"You ought to visit the old factory near my house," Tracy went on. "There's toxic waste buried there."

I didn't have time to ask Tracy any questions. Mr. Barron's voice boomed across the gym.

"We've got lots to do tonight," he was saying. "I'm sure that you all worked extra hard over Christmas vacation and have a lot of memory work to recite."

A collective groan went up from the group, and my heart sank. I'd been so busy putting models together and playing outside, I'd forgotten my Awana assignment. Well, that was another thing I'd have to be more accountable for in the new year.

Mom was folding clothes in the kitchen when I got home. "So, did you talk to Aunt Kathy, huh?" I badgered her.

She laughed. "Yes, I did. She thinks it's a terrific idea. She suggested you take the commuter train to the city and she'll meet you. Then you can come back together and she'll have dinner with us. You can do it on the teacher institute day next week. You don't have school."

"You mean I can take the train alone?" I asked.

"Well, you did so well on the bus trip to visit your dad, I don't see why you can't ride twenty-five miles on a commuter train," she said.

"Man, that'll be neat!" I said. "I could carry a briefcase like all the commuters I see at the Grandville station."

"She'll meet you at the other end," explained Mom, "and the two of you will take a taxi to her library."

I could hardly contain myself. Not only would I be able to do the best report I'd ever done, but I'd get to ride the train to Chicago and take a taxi. Ever since we'd moved here, I'd wondered what it would be like to ride the train. As I watched the trains rush to the city, I'd imagined sitting behind the tinted windows.

"I think you've had enough excitement for tonight, Josh," Mom said. "It's time to hit the sack."

I gave her a quick hug and kiss and almost skipped off to bed.

I had lots to talk to God about before I went to sleep. But first, I was going to read my Bible. Since I'd met Jesus and asked Him into my heart back in

October, I hadn't read my Bible very much. It was hard to understand. But I was going to try what Mr. Barron had suggested, reading ten verses each night starting in the book of Matthew. He'd given me a Living Bible that was easier to understand. He said I'd learn a lot of interesting stuff about Jesus.

I opened the Bible and found the book of Matthew and began reading. By the time I reached the third verse, my eyes were beginning to cross. "Judah was the father of Perez and Zerah (Tamar was their mother); Perez was the father of Hezron; Hezron was the father of Aram." It reminded me of the tongue twister my dad recited when I was little, "Peter Piper picked a peck of pickled peppers."

But I was determined. I skipped all of the long names and started reading again further on. I didn't think God would mind.

I was so excited about the prospect of a trip to Chicago, I knew I wouldn't fall asleep while I was praying tonight.

Dear God, I prayed, *Thank you for answering some of my prayers. I don't understand some of the stuff I read in the Bible, but maybe You can figure that out. Bless my dad tonight.*

I wondered if he still went over to his friend Sally's house. I hoped not. She couldn't cook as good as my mom, and Dad had looked pretty thin when I visited at Thanksgiving.

God, I still don't know what to do about Sonny and my mom. He's my friend and not hers. I found him first. And besides, mothers aren't supposed to go out on dates with guys. They're just supposed to be mothers.

My mom was pretty, though. A lot prettier than Sally. I wondered why Dad didn't like her anymore. Grown-ups sure are hard to figure.

God, please help me understand my parents. I really want them to get back together again so we can be a family. Amen.

So far, the new year was okay, I thought as I turned out the light by my bed. I wasn't in any major trouble, and I had a trip to look forward to. Wait until Wendell found out. He loved libraries. He'd really be jealous.

Nah, Wendell probably wouldn't be jealous. He never seemed to have any bad feelings. He'd just be happy for me. It was disgusting how good Wendell was.

I dreaded the thought of facing Sonny at work after school. But Mrs. Bannister had lots of things planned for the day, so I didn't have time to worry.

One of the garbage groups was doing something special. They'd been whispering and laughing about it this morning on the playground. It promised to be a change from our regular Thursday routine.

We were also starting a new unit in Language Arts—something about writing a letter to an imaginary character.

And then what I'd been waiting for—a conference with Mrs. Bannister about my research report. She was meeting with each student to talk about their ideas. She wasn't kidding about this accountability stuff. But this time I was ready for her. I had my library trip all planned, and I had an idea in mind. We'd talked more about toxic waste in class, and I'd walked past the site at the old factory that Tracy had told me about. It was surrounded by an eight-foot fence and lots of danger signs.

Mrs. Bannister was trying to get our attention. "Class, it's time for language arts. We're starting our letter-writing unit today."

The minute she said the word "letter" I began thinking about Dad. He hadn't written me since Thanksgiving, though I'd written a thank-you letter after my visit. Mom had made me do it right away so I wouldn't forget.

"We're going to be writing to imaginary characters," explained Mrs. Bannister.

Well, that left Dad out of the picture. He was real, all right. I'd seen and touched him at Thanksgiving.

"You can choose any imaginary character," Mrs. Bannister went on. "It could be someone from a comic strip, a cartoon character from TV, or a character from a book you've read."

My mind began to consider the possibilities. Superman, Dennis the Menace, Henry Reed, Encyclopedia Brown. Then it hit me. Why not write to McGee? McGee was a cartoon guy we watched on videos at Awana sometimes. I wouldn't mind having someone like him for a friend. He seemed more real than any other imaginary character. Maybe I could even mail the letter to McGee's creator, if Mr. Barron had an address.

Mrs. Bannister completed her instructions. "You must include at least two things in your letter—some information about yourself that you think the character would want to know and two questions you'd like the character to answer about himself or herself."

Usually it took me a little while to get an idea for a writing assignment, but today my mind was racing.

Dear McGee,

You don't know me, but I know you. I've seen your videos at my Awana Club. I think you're terrific. My name is Joshua McIntire and I'm ten years old. My teacher is making us write a letter to an imaginary character, and I picked you because you're so cool.

My mom and dad are divorced. Mom and I moved to this town last fall. It's a pretty good place to live, except I've gotten in a lot of trouble here. I didn't get into trouble in my old school.

I'm trying to be better this year and I think it will work because God is helping me now. I became a Christian in October. It's not as easy as I thought it would be. At least not as easy as my friend Wendell makes it look. Wendell is a Christian too. That's how I got to be a Christian, because Wendell witnessed to me.

I need to know some stuff about you. How old are you? What kind of sports do you like? Do you have a girlfriend? I don't really have a girlfriend except I do like Tracy. She has red hair and wears glasses. She goes to Awana too, but I've never had the nerve to tell her I'm a Christian.

Please answer right away. I just know I'm the only person who will get a reply.

> Sincerely,
> Joshua McIntire

I raised my hand when I was finished.

Mrs. Bannister quickly came over to my desk. "Well, I'm impressed, Joshua," she said. "You finished that assignment in record time. You took my lecture on being accountable quite seriously."

"I need to mail this right away," I said.

She looked puzzled. "We're writing to imaginary characters," she said. "That means they only exist in the imagination of someone else. Where in the world would you send it?"

I explained about Awana and Mr. Barron, and she smiled. "Well, it's okay with me," she said. "I'll read it right now."

"It's kind of personal," I said with embarrassment.

"I'll keep everything confidential, Josh," she assured me.

She quickly read my letter. "You've done a marvelous job, Joshua," she said. "That's an A paper."

She hurried to her desk and put my grade in the book. A warm glow spread over me. Getting good grades made me feel so good, I wondered why I didn't try harder all the time.

It was lunch recess, and the temperature was warmer. Maybe spring was coming early this year. I unzipped my jacket.

I noticed Trevor standing near a group of third graders. Something about the way he looked made me feel uneasy. I walked over in his direction.

"You're a dumb bunny," I heard one of them say to Trevor.

"Yeah," taunted another. "You look funny."

I rushed to Trevor's side just in time to see a big tear roll down his cheek.

"You kids don't know what you're talking about!" I shouted at them. "Trevor's my friend." I was angry and felt like karate chopping both of them. But I remembered Master Lee's advice about when to use karate, and this wasn't one of those times.

I put my arm around Trevor's shoulder. "Are you okay?" I asked.

He nodded.

"They're the dumb ones," I said. "You helped me out of a jam in class the other day when I wasn't listening," I reminded him. "If you were dumb, you wouldn't have been able to do that."

He gave me one of his big smiles. "I like you, Josh," he said.

"And I like you, Trevor," I answered. "We can handle those puny third graders, can't we?"

Trevor nodded uncertainly.

"C'mon," I said, "let's shoot baskets."

But the bell rang and we rushed to line up.

It was time for our first garbage project. Somebody had pushed all the desks back against the walls while we were gone. The chairs were arranged in rows in the center of the room. This looked interesting.

"Mrs. Swanson's first-grade class is going to join us in a minute," Mrs. Bannister announced. "Sit on the counter or one of the desktops. The first graders get the chairs."

It was Ben's group that was going first. You could never tell what he was going to come up with. I hoped Mrs. Bannister knew what was going on.

Just then Ben and Samantha brought two huge garbage bags into the classroom. They looked just like the ones we used for lunch trash. Ben spread out a plastic drop cloth at the front of the room. This was really a weird project.

There was a knock on the door, and the first graders filed in. They looked a little confused as Mrs. Swanson got them seated in the big chairs. Boy, were they tiny.

Mrs. Bannister motioned for Ben to begin. I couldn't believe that she was actually letting him take charge. Ben opened up a garbage bag and with a flourish dumped it on the floor. Thank goodness for the drop cloth. Half-empty milk cartons, clumps of leftover spaghetti, banana peels, bread crusts, and crumpled-up potato chip wrappers formed a disgusting pile. It was not a pretty sight, and it smelled even worse.

I looked over at Mrs. Bannister. She didn't seem at all alarmed. Could this have been planned in advance? Then Samantha dumped her bag onto the pile. She wasn't having as much fun as Ben. I could tell by the look on her face.

Samantha started. "This is all of the garbage that you guys threw away at lunch time," she explained, pointing at the first graders. The little kids looked really confused now. Why in the world would somebody save their garbage?

"We're going to show you how to bring lunches that won't make so much garbage, because we're running out of places in the world to put it."

She was doing a good job. The first graders looked like they understood what she was saying.

Darrin, the third member of the group, talked about the importance of packing lunches from home in plastic containers instead of using wrapping paper that made more garbage.

"It's even a good idea," he said, "to bring your lunch in a cloth bag or lunch box instead of a paper bag."

I noticed he stayed far away from the garbage heap while he was talking. But Ben just stuck his hand right in and picked out things that could be recycled. It was a pretty impressive act. Pop cans, lunch trays, yogurt containers.

"Our group is going to try to start a recycling program at Jefferson," he explained.

Samantha put on some plastic gloves for her part of the program. No way was she going to touch any of that garbage with her bare hands.

"See these containers?" she pointed out. "Some manufacturers pack things in tons of cardboard and plastic that can't be recycled. Tell your mom not to buy them. They make too much garbage and won't dissolve in a garbage dump for hundreds of years."

Maria finished up the presentation, and Mrs. Swanson led her class in applause. She thanked the group, and the first graders were on their way.

I hoped Ben's group wasn't going to leave that pile up in the front of the room all afternoon. But I had to admit it had been a pretty impressive performance. How could our group top that?

There was just time for a few conferences on our research reports before recess. My hand shot up when Mrs. Bannister asked for volunteers. She called me to the round table at the back of the room.

"Here you are first again, Joshua," she said. "You must have an idea already."

I told her excitedly about going to the university library in Chicago to do research on toxic waste. She caught my enthusiasm and asked several questions.

By the time we'd finished I felt ready. My report would be about the best ways to clean up toxic waste sites—and it would be the best piece of work I'd ever done.

Wow! This had been a bell-ringer of a day. That's an expression my dad always used when he'd had a good day. Thinking of Dad made me wonder again why he didn't write or call. I was his only kid, and it wouldn't take that much time.

I was halfway toward home when I remembered that it was Thursday—which meant I was due at the leather shop. The good feelings I'd had just minutes before vanished. What would I say to Sonny? I stopped short in my tracks and turned to Wendell.

"See ya," I said with a long face.

"Where ya going?" he asked.

"Today's my day to work at the leather shop," I explained.

"How come you look so sad?" he asked. "I thought you liked it there."

I hadn't talked to Wendell much lately about what I was thinking. We'd just been too busy. Maybe he'd have some good advice. I explained about Sonny asking my mom out.

"Boy, that's a tough problem," he said. "Why would Sonny want to ask your mom out on a date?"

"Beats me," I said. "It sure does complicate things."

"Well," said Wendell, "I wouldn't know what to do." Wendell usually had the answers to everything.

Oddly enough I felt better.

"But you know what I do when I don't have the answer?" he went on. "I pray."

Somehow I should have known that's what he would say.

"You go to work," said Wendell, "and I'll pray for you. You'll figure something out. I know you will."

I wished I had Wendell's faith.

Sonny was cutting leather at the big counter in the front of the store. A cassette that his band had recorded was playing softly in the boom box. It was one of my favorite songs. Sonny stopped what he was doing and stuck out his hand.

"Howdy, pardner," he said.

I awkwardly put out my hand.

"Hey, what's the matter?" He tousled my hair with his hand.

I pulled away.

"There is a problem, isn't there?" he continued.

"Yeah," I said.

"So, tell me about it."

I didn't know where to begin. I stood and stared

at him with a blank face.

Suddenly his face lit up. "Ah, I think I've figured it out," he said. "It's your mom, isn't it?"

Once the words were out, I couldn't hold back. I started to cry again.

"Aw, c'mon, Josh, I'm sorry," he said. "I thought you'd like it if I was nice to your mom."

"But you're my friend," I blubbered. "If you go out with my mom you'll be her friend. And you'll tell her all the stuff we talk about."

"I wouldn't do that," Sonny said.

"And besides," I said, "moms don't go out on dates."

Sonny laughed.

"I don't get what's so funny," I said.

"Moms who are divorced go out on dates," Sonny explained. "They're not married anymore, so it's all right."

"Well, I don't care. My mom doesn't go out on dates." My voice was getting a little louder. This was turning into an argument, not a discussion.

"Josh, I'm sorry about the way I've made you feel. You're my friend, and I wouldn't want to do anything to hurt you. But your mom is a really nice lady," he went on, "and I'm single."

"I know she's nice," I said. "But she belongs to me." There. I'd said it. I wanted my mom to myself and Sonny to myself. I didn't want to share them.

Once I'd spoken the words out loud, I felt better.

"I was wondering why she said no," he continued. "Now I understand."

"She said no?" I asked.

"Yeah, she said no," he answered. "Really bruised my ego too. I haven't had too many pretty ladies refuse a dinner invitation from Sonny Studebaker."

I gave him a big smile. Maybe things would turn out all right after all.

I picked up the broom and started sweeping up the leather pieces that had fallen to the floor.

It was dark outside when I woke up Monday morning, and the illuminated dial on my alarm clock said 4:00. Two more hours until it would ring.

I'd never been to Chicago before. I hadn't ever ridden a train.

It seemed like Mom had gone over the instructions with me about fifty times. She was going to drive me to the commuter station where we'd buy my round-trip ticket. I'd use half on the way in and half on the way back. My mom would watch while I got on the train and found a seat. I had strict instructions to stay in that seat until the train pulled into Chicago. And I wasn't supposed to talk to strangers. My aunt would be waiting for me when I got off the train.

It sounded simple enough. I couldn't figure out why my mom was getting so bent out of shape.

I must have fallen asleep again, because the alarm woke me at six. Mom had allowed plenty of time for breakfast before the 7:11 train. I got washed and dressed in record time. I wasn't sure I'd be able to eat anything. I had that fluttering feeling I get in my stomach whenever I'm excited.

"Let's go over the instructions one more time," Mom said, as she poured a glass of orange juice for me.

"Aw, Mom," I replied, "I've traveled alone before."

"Well, aren't you the confident one this morning?" she teased.

"I'm not a baby," I reminded her.

"How well I know," she laughed. "You've grown up a lot since we moved to Grandville."

After breakfast I checked over the contents of my book bag. It wasn't a briefcase, but it would have to do.

Mom gave me a five-dollar bill.

"What's this for?" I asked.

"Just in case of an emergency," she said.

"What kind of emergency?" I wondered.

"That's the definition of emergency," she explained. "It's something you can't predict. But you'll be fine. I'm putting you on the train, and Aunt Kathy is taking you off. If you don't need the money, you can use it to buy a souvenir."

It took Mom awhile to scrape the ice and snow

45

from her car windows. I tried to help, but we only had one scraper. Then we were off to the station. Now it felt like I had a whole colony of butterflies in my stomach.

We pulled into the commuter parking lot, crowded with cars and people. The darkness made it feel like the middle of the night. Wow, there were a lot of people who worked in Chicago.

Mom paid for my ticket and we went outside on the platform to wait. People were balancing coffee cups and reading newspapers. Nobody talked to each other. Maybe they were still sleepy. I noticed lots of people wearing gym shoes. Did they have gym classes at their offices?

"Now, Josh," Mom began. I could tell she was going to go over the instructions one more time.

"Mom," I pleaded. "I know what to do. Okay?"

"All right," she agreed. "Have a wonderful time. I'll pick you and Aunt Kathy up at 5:34."

Where did they get those weird times that the trains came and went, anyway—7:11 and 5:34?

I could see the spotlight on the engine off in the distance before I heard the rumbling. I was used to the vibrations the commuter trains made as they roared through Grandville. Jefferson School was on the other side of the tracks. But close up the train was awesome. The minute it stopped, the quiet crowd came alive. They started running and pushing and shoving. It reminded me of the playground at recess when the bell rang.

Mom gave me a quick kiss. "I'll watch from right here while you find a seat. Wave to me from the window and I'll know you're okay," she instructed.

A conductor reached out to help me up the steps, and I made my way into one of the cars. There were two levels of seats. Mom and I hadn't talked about this. I decided I'd better take the lower level where she could see me. I spotted her standing alone on the platform. She looked tiny. I waved and she blew me a kiss. I hoped no one had noticed.

The conductor shouted, "All aboard for Chicago. Please have your tickets ready." And then the train pulled out. I looked out the window to wave at Mom again, but she was already gone. My trip to Chicago had begun.

No one was sitting next to me, so I put my book bag on the seat. It was quiet in the car. Most people reading their newspapers. Some people even had Walkmans on.

"I need to see your ticket, son." The conductor was standing in the aisle beside me. I pulled it out of my pocket. He punched it and slipped it under a clip on the seat in front of me. So that's how he'd remember that I had paid for my ticket.

I watched the world flying by through the window. The sky was beginning to lighten as the sun came up.

Cars were lined up at the railroad crossings waiting for the train to pass. Their lights looked like eyes blinking up at me. We went past LaVeen's Lumber Yard, and I remembered running along the train tracks here when I first came to Grandville. That seemed like years ago.

All of a sudden the train began to slow down. Then it stopped. What was going on? We couldn't be in Chicago already. I heard the conductor's voice call out, "Westbury, this stop is Westbury." Crowds of people waiting on the platform in Westbury rushed onto the train.

Somebody stood beside my seat and frowned on my book bag. I got the message and moved it to the floor. The person sat down. She didn't look like any commuter I'd ever seen. Her black hair was spiked, she had feathered earrings that were at least five inches long, and her fingernails were painted a fluorescent pink. She was carrying a large portfolio. She slipped off her leather jacket and sighed deeply.

"So where ya goin', kid?" she asked me.

I was sure she qualified as a stranger. At least I'd never seen anybody stranger in all my life. At school, the teachers always talked about "Mr. Stranger Danger," but there wasn't a category for "Ms. Stranger Danger."

I decided to take the plunge.

"Chicago," I said.

"So, what's your name?" Ms. Danger asked.

"Josh," I replied.

"Mine's Louanne," she volunteered. Louanne

seemed like a pretty normal name for this exotic-looking creature. "I'm a student at the Art Institute," she went on. "Right now I've got to finish an assignment. S'cuse." She pulled a ragged paperback out of her portfolio and began to read.

I shifted my body in the seat and turned to the window. We were passing a football stadium. The field was covered with snow, but there were runners moving around the track. They were bundled up against the chill.

The train seemed to shift from side to side as we moved forward, and I had to brace myself to keep from bumping Louanne. The man across the aisle seemed to be sleeping. How did he keep from falling over?

Suddenly Louanne shoved her paperback into the portfolio. "Now I can relax," she said. "My homework's done." She looked me over. "How come you're not in school?"

"It's a teacher institute day and I'm meeting my aunt in Chicago," I explained.

"Cool," she said. "I love the city. I'd move there tomorrow if I could afford it. I can't stand my parents."

I looked at her in surprise. I didn't know people didn't like their parents.

"Why?" I blurted out without thinking.

But Louanne didn't seem to find it strange.

"All they do is rag on me," she said. "Don't do

this, do that. It drives me crazy."

I didn't know how to reply to that revelation, so I waited. She didn't pause for long.

"They don't like what I wear, they don't like my friends, they think I stay out too late." Her list seemed to go on forever.

"Can you believe they don't even like my hairdo?" She pointed to the jet-black spikes that looked dangerously sharp.

Yes, I could believe they didn't like it. I thought it was pretty weird myself, but I wasn't going to say so.

She didn't seem to expect any reply. Maybe it was one of those "rhetorical questions" that Mrs. Bannister told us about. She said if someone asks a "rhetorical question," you aren't supposed to answer it.

Louanne was on a roll now. "Furthermore," she said, shaking her fluorescent finger to punctuate her comments, "they think my boyfriend is a jerk."

Wow, did Louanne ever have problems. Mine seemed minor in comparison.

"So, what about you?"

I wasn't sure I wanted to tell her about me. I didn't even know her. But I didn't want to be rude. In fact, I kind of liked her.

"My parents are divorced," I said.

"Mine might as well be," she offered. "All they ever do is fight."

"Mine didn't ever fight at all," I said. "One day

my dad just left. I don't get to see him very much."

"Hey," she encouraged, "you gotta roll with the punches."

I didn't know what she meant.

"You gotta keep your chin up."

Now I understood.

The conductor was calling out in a sing-song voice, "Chicago, we are pulling into the North-western Station in Chicago. Take your monthly passes with you, ladies and gentlemen. And have a pleasant day."

"So, it was nice to meet you, Josh. Hope things work out okay." Louanne stuck out her hand. I shook it, hoping I wouldn't get stabbed by a fingernail.

The train lurched to a stop.

"Bye." Louanne dashed down the aisle before the rest of the passengers were even standing. Clearly she found a system that worked.

Suddenly I was alone. My instructions were foggy. Did I go out the front or the back of the car? I followed the man across the aisle. He looked wide awake now.

The conductor helped me down the steps. I looked around for my aunt, but she wasn't there. There were just crowds of people rushing down the platform. Now I saw why they needed to wear gym shoes.

I decided to follow everybody else. They seemed to know where they were going. The platform ended, and the crowd moved through a set of automatic double doors. We were inside the station. I felt like an ant about to be crushed, and I stepped aside so I wouldn't get trampled.

The commuters shot off in six different directions. There were escalators going up, escalators going down, hallways going left, and hallways going right. I still didn't see my aunt. For the first time I began to worry. I reviewed the instructions in my mind. I could remember nothing about taking escalators or going down hallways. My mom specifically said my aunt would be waiting for me when I got off the train. I was now off the train. Where was she?

And now I had a more serious problem. I had to go to the bathroom. But if I went to the bathroom, I might miss my aunt. And my mom was always warning me about public restrooms. She said they were dirty and weirdos hung out there.

Now what? I paced back and forth for a few minutes. I had no choice. I didn't think my mom would want me to have an accident in the middle of Northwestern Station.

There were signs everywhere: To Taxi Stand, To Monroe Street, Newsstand, Delicatessen. But I couldn't see a single sign that said "Boys." I'd have to find it soon.

Then I spied it. The sign said "Gentlemen." I didn't care what it was called, I just needed to go. I hurried across the station and pulled open the door. It was a heavy wooden one. There was no one around. I breathed a sigh of relief.

While I was washing my hands, the door opened. The man who came in looked like a commuter.

"You're a good-looking young man. Can I buy you something to eat?" He was talking to me.

My heart stopped. I didn't need a neon sign to tell me that this was "Mr. Stranger Danger." But he looked so nice. He was wearing shoes with little tassels on them and tortoise-shell glasses like my dad's.

I felt like my feet were glued to the ceramic tiles.

The man stood between me and the door. He smiled and spoke again. "You're alone, aren't you?"

I could hear my heart pounding. It sounded like jungle drums. I needed to do something fast. I had to get out of here. I walked toward the door, and he didn't move. Then, somehow, I found my running legs and darted around him. The door pushed outward and I burst into the station. I didn't know where I was going, but I kept on moving.

The delicatessen's doors were open and I sprinted through them. I didn't see the clerk standing in the shadows, and the bulk of his body stopped me short.

"Hey, where you headin'?" he asked.

Between short gasps for breath, I managed to tell my story. His uniform, even though it was just an apron and hat, made me feel safe.

"I'm going to call security," he said. "You look like you could use a cup of hot chocolate."

He motioned for me to sit at the counter, and I climbed up on a stool. I could hear him explaining what had happened to someone on the telephone. Then he hung up and brought me a mug. There were piles of whipped cream on top, and I began to feel safe once again.

I whispered a fast thank you prayer. I hadn't had time to pray in the bathroom. But God helped me out anyhow. *Thanks, God. It's great to have You on my side.*

The security policeman wasn't a policeman at all. She was a girl. But she was wearing a gun and carrying a radio that was crackling and calling. I was glad to have her on my side too.

"Tell me what happened," she said.

I told my story again.

"What are you doing wandering around the station by yourself?" she asked.

"My aunt was supposed to meet me," I explained. "But she didn't come."

"Here's what we're going to do," she told me. "I'm putting out an all-call for the man fitting your description. Then I'm going to ask the station manager to page your aunt. Maybe she's here looking for you."

I breathed a sigh of relief. "Where do I go now?" I asked.

"Come with me. You can wait in the manager's office until we find your aunt. Don't worry."

I left my mug of cocoa and followed her out of the deli. I glanced around the station, but I still didn't see Aunt Kathy. What if something had happened to her?

We took the escalator up. The sun shone through a skylight and sparkled on a giant silver sculpture suspended from the ceiling. It turned slowly.

This was really a neat place. The manager's office was pretty impressive, too. Nothing like Mom's at Associated Foods where she was a secretary.

Bennett (that's what the policewoman's name-plate read) got me a Coke and settled me in a chair. The windows reached from floor to ceiling. Dozens of skyscrapers dotted the edge of a river spanned by several large bridges. Maybe I could be a station manager when I grew up.

Bennett came back with a big smile on her face. "Good news, Josh," she said. "We've found both the man who was bothering you and your aunt. The man is being questioned, and your aunt is waiting down-stairs." I was impressed with her efficiency. Maybe girls did make good policemen. I mentally corrected myself—good policewomen.

Once again I had to leave my refreshments unfinished. First the cocoa, now the Coke. But I was anxious to see Aunt Kathy.

She was waiting at the bottom of the escalator and looked like she'd been crying. "Oh, Joshua, I was frantic. Are you okay?"

I nodded. "I'm fine," I said. "Are you okay?"

"Yes," she said. "Just as my taxi got to the river, the bridge went up to let some boats through. I was stranded." She gave me a big hug and kiss.

All this mushy stuff was a little embarrassing, but I was so glad to see her, I hugged her right back.

Aunt Kathy didn't look anything like you'd expect a professor to look. She was pretty and didn't even wear glasses.

"You two seem all right now," said the policewoman. "I'll just get back to work."

"Did you ask her to help you when you couldn't find me?" Aunt Kathy asked.

"Well," I hesitated. "There's a little more."

Now she really looked alarmed. Bit by bit she wormed the story out of me.

"Your mother is going to kill me," she said.

"No," I said. "I think she's going to kill me."

She laughed. "Well, we'll just have to protect each other then."

For the first time since I'd left home that morning, I relaxed.

"We'd better get moving," she said. "We have lots to do today."

This time we took the escalator going down. Instead of a sculpture, there was a giant kite suspended overhead. I stared up at the colorful display and almost lost my footing as the escalator ended.

"We're going to take a taxi to my library," explained Aunt Kathy. "I don't have a car."

"How do you get anywhere?" I wondered.

"Public transportation," she answered. "Buses, trains, taxis, the el."

"What's the el?" I asked.

"Oh, it's great," she said. "Sometimes it goes under the ground and sometimes it runs up in the air on tracks that look like they're built on stilts."

There was a lot to learn about living in the city. We jumped into a yellow taxi cab. It smelled like cabbage and the driver looked like someone from an adventure movie. I was glad Aunt Kathy was in charge now.

"Michigan and Congress," she instructed the driver.

We pulled away from the curb with a squeal across three lanes of traffic. Maybe we were part of an adventure movie and I didn't know it.

"So, tell me about this research project you're working on," my aunt said. "I'm pretty impressed that you're doing this kind of thing in the fifth grade. I didn't start doing research until I got to college."

I smiled. "I want to find out about toxic waste sites and how to get rid of them," I said. "We've got one in Grandville and I think we should get rid of it."

"That sounds like an ambitious project for a ten year old, but I'm game if you are," she said. "If we can't find the answer in my library, we can't find it anywhere."

The taxi pulled up in front of a dingy-looking building.

"This is it," Aunt Kathy said. "It doesn't look like much, but we have more books than any other library in the city." She paid the driver, and he screeched off again.

The library was bright and modern inside. We went through a turnstile and my aunt showed a guard her identification pass. There were more escalators, both up and down. No one in the city used stairs, it seemed.

"We'll put our coats in my locker," she explained. "I work here so often, I just rent one."

We took the escalator down to the lower level. Everywhere I looked there were shelves of books. They stretched from ceiling to floor.

"How do you reach the books on the top shelves?" I asked.

"Oh, there are step-stools," she explained. "But we don't get too many kids here." She laughed. "I'll help you."

We stashed our stuff in the locker and were on our way.

"Our first stop is the computerized card catalog," she said. "That's where we'll find out what the library has on your subject."

"What's a computerized card catalog?" I asked. The card catalogs at school and the public library were in drawers.

"This library has so many books," she explained, "that instead of thumbing through drawers to look for titles, we just type in the subject and let the computer do the work."

"Cool," I said. I was glad she was with me. It was too confusing for a kid.

There were stools clustered around dozens of computer terminals. We found an empty one and I hopped up.

"So, Joshua," she said, "what subjects do you think we should type in?"

"Well," I said, "toxic waste is one."

"Good. We'll start with that and see where it leads us. Looking for things in the card catalog is like being a detective. Who knows what we'll find?"

I wished Wendell were with me. He was the only kid I knew who would really appreciate a computerized card catalog. Wait until I told him about my day. My aunt's fingers flew over the keyboard. The computer seemed to be thinking for a second, then the screen filled up with words.

"I think we've found what we're looking for," said my aunt. "There are some books, a lot of magazines, and a few government documents."

"What are those?" I asked.

"They're published by the United States government and have to do with official business," she explained. "We'll start with the magazines since they're the most up-to-date."

She was off and running again. I was glad I'd worn my gym shoes.

"We're going to the periodical room now. That's what we call magazines in the library," she said.

It was close to lunch time before we'd found everything she wanted. We had covered five floors and ridden the escalator up and down so many times I was dizzy. Research was harder work than I thought.

"Well, Joshua, are you ready for some lunch?" she asked.

"I'm starving," I said.

"Well, we're not eating at Fond du la Tour," she

said, "but you won't go hungry."

I had no idea what Fond du la Tour was, but I was glad to hear I wouldn't starve.

We took the escalator back down to a room filled with vending machines.

"No waitresses in this restaurant," she said. She pulled out a change purse stuffed with quarters and dimes. "Just wander around and see what looks good."

I'd never seen anything like it before. One machine was filled with chips and snacks. Another held sandwiches. The candy bar machine was the best. It had Paydays, Kit Kats, and Peanut M & Ms. All my favorites. Plus there were milk, pop, juice, ice cream, fruit. The only thing missing was vegetables. There was even a machine that dispensed coins when you put in dollar bills. Maybe I could talk to Mrs. Raymond about getting these for our lunchroom. It would be a big improvement over the cafeteria lunches.

After lunch we spread out the books and magazines we'd collected on a table. Aunt Kathy helped me sort through them.

"Start by reading this article, Josh," she suggested. "I think it will give you some good ideas for your report."

I'd been worried that the stuff would be too hard, but it wasn't. The author was talking about the toxic waste site in Grandville. He gave a lot of good suggestions for cleaning it up. I wondered why nobody had ever done anything about it.

"Let's photocopy this one," Aunt Kathy said.

"Why can't we just take it with us?" I asked.

"In big research libraries, periodicals are never checked out. We'll just make a copy."

She pulled a card from her purse and inserted it in the copy machine. "This way I don't have to carry so much change with me. The vending machines are bad enough."

I was going to be ready for college after this day. Maybe I could bring Wendell down here and help him with his report too.

We took another escalator down to the checkout.

"Hello, Dr. Norton." The girl behind the desk was one of my aunt's students.

Aunt Kathy introduced me as her nephew from the suburbs. I felt proud.

"We've got time for a little sightseeing before we catch the train," my aunt said. "Where would you like to go?"

"Could we go to Soldier Field?" I asked.

"What in the world for?"

"That's where the Bears play," I explained.

"How about a sports memorabilia store?" she suggested. "Would that be okay instead?"

I had no idea what a sports memorabilia store would

have in it, but I nodded in agreement.

"They've got hats and shirts and mugs from all of the Chicago teams," she told me.

Now I knew how I would spend that five-dollar bill Mom had given me.

Since my trip to the city to visit Aunt Kathy, I'd done nothing but read about toxic waste. It was pretty depressing. I'd found out that there were lots of places in the country that had poisonous chemicals left over from when we didn't know as much about the environment.

I read old newspapers in the Grandville public library and found out that some people had tried a few years ago to get rid of the site, but their plan fizzled when they ran out of money. I knew what I was going to do—write the governor a letter. I'd gotten an A on that letter I wrote to McGee. Why couldn't I write the governor a letter too?

I borrowed some stationery from Mom. Notebook paper was okay for McGee, but I wanted to impress the governor. I spent all of my journal-writing periods for a whole week working on the letter. Finally it was perfect.

Dear Governor Henry,

My name is Joshua McIntire and I live in Grandville. I am in fifth grade. Maybe you don't know about our town, but it has a toxic waste site. An old factory used bad chemicals to manufacture things a long time ago, and when they closed the factory they left the chemicals there. They are dangerous for the children of our town. You are the only person who can help us get rid of them.

I am doing a science report on toxic waste and I read that you are concerned about the environment. If you do care, you should come to Grandville and visit the site. I will be glad to show you where it is. Please write and let me know when you are coming.

Sincerely,
Joshua McIntire

I dropped the letter in the out-of-town box at the post office. I wasn't taking any chances.

In the days that followed, I went to karate and Awana and I worked for Sonny. But all the while I was thinking about my science project and the governor. I even prayed that the governor would pay attention to my letter.

"Joshua, don't you think you're taking this toxic waste thing a little too seriously?" Mom asked one night.

We were eating dinner together. She had fixed

lasagna and garlic bread.

"Whaddya mean?" I asked.

"Well, all you talk about is toxic waste. It's not the most appealing subject in the whole world. I'd just as soon forget it exists," she said.

"But that's the problem with you adults," I complained. "You're not thinking about us kids and the world we're going to inherit."

"You sound pretty grown up for a fifth grader," she said. "Where are you getting these ideas?"

"From all the stuff I've been reading," I said.

"Well, I don't want you to be too disappointed," she said. "I'd be shocked if the governor had time for a fifth grader in Grandville."

Wendell was picking me up in fifteen minutes for Awana. I was getting some badges that night, and I could hardly wait. I finished the last of my math problems just before the doorbell rang.

"Hi, Wen," I said. "Just a sec while I grab my stuff."

"I oughtta be hearing from the governor any day now," I said as we headed for church.

"Aw, you don't really think he'll write you, do you?" Wendell said.

Nobody had any faith in my powers of persuasion.

"Yeah, Wendell, I do," I answered.

"Well, what are you going to do if he doesn't?" he asked.

"I'll write him another letter," I said. "I'm not

going to quit on this."

"Man, you're serious, aren't you?"

I certainly was.

On Wednesday I rushed home from school and checked the mailbox. Jackpot. There were three envelopes inside, all addressed to Joshua McIntire. My hands were shaking as I checked the return addresses. One was from Dad, one was from McGee, and the third was a thick creamy white envelope embossed with the governor's seal.

I knew which one I'd open first. I held my breath while I read the governor's letter.

Dear Joshua,

Thank you very much for your letter about the toxic waste site in Grandville. I agree with you about the dangers of having such a site in your town. I would like to make a visit there soon to inspect the location so I can instruct my advisors about what to do. I would be honored to have you be my escort. My assistant will be calling your school sometime next week to make arrangements.

Again, thank you and I look forward to meeting you soon.

Sincerely,
Thomas Henry
The Honorable Governor of the State of Illinois

70

Even though I'd been so sure it would happen, I couldn't believe it. The governor was actually coming to see me in Grandville. Would he come to Jefferson? Would Mrs. Bannister mark me absent? Dozens of questions raced through my mind. I'd have to get a haircut before he came.

I had two more letters to open. Which one next? I decided that McGee could wait. I hoped he wouldn't mind, but I hadn't heard from Dad since Thanksgiving.

Dear Josh,

Hope you're doing okay. I'm still working and living in the same places. That's good news. Sally says hi to you. We're still friends. I'm glad you liked the models I sent you for Christmas. I got your thank-you letter. You write a good letter.

I couldn't wait to tell Dad what good letters I really did write. I got the governor to write me back.

I'm going to be coming back to Woodview to take care of some business. Ask your mom if I could stop by to see you. I'd like to take you out for a meal and bowling.

Wow, this was a red-letter day. Not only was the governor coming, but my dad was coming too. I couldn't contain my excitement. I wasn't supposed to call Mom at the office, but I had to talk to somebody.

I'll call later with some dates, but I've got to go to work now. See you soon.

Love, Dad

I still had one more letter to open. The return address just said McGee, but the postmark was Thousand Oaks, California. I'd never heard of it before. The letter was typewritten on plain white paper.

Hey Josho:

What a tremendously terrific treat tearing into your letter to me today. (Say that seven times fast.) After another rough afternoon of saving the earth from thermal nuclear destruction (let alone emptying the family cat box), it was great to kick back and read some fan mail.

Glad you like my videos. When me and Nick aren't out in Hollywood filming my adventurous adventures, we're at home writing them in books (which are even better, 'cause I get to tell them in my own wonderfully wondrous words).

Sorry to hear about your folks' divorce. A lot of that going around these days. The trick is to remember they still love you. As a cartoon character I really don't have parents, unless you count Nicholas who dreamed me up on his sketch pad back in 1989. (I still don't know why he only gave me eight fingers and eight toes but, hey, he's an artist, not a mathematician.) I keep bugging him to draw me a beautiful babe—you know, a McGette—so we can have a bunch of little McGeeites toddling around. He says, "No way, one of you is enough."

It's cool that ol' Wendell told you about Jesus and that

you decided to let Him be the boss of your life. Nick made that decision a few years back. It won't always be easy, but it's the smartest move you'll ever make.

Well, it's getting late. Think I'll hop back into my sketch pad, swim a few laps in my Olympic size pool (hey, it's a big sketch pad), and call it a night.

Thanks for the note, and anytime you want to say hi or low (hee, hee, that's a little cartoon humor), just drop me a line.

Your friend,
McGee

I bet nobody else in 5B will get a reply to their letter, I thought. I had to call Mom and tell her the good news.

"Associated Foods, Mr. Terpstra's office." My mom answered the phone in her usual cheerful voice.

"I know I'm not supposed to bother you at work, but I've got to talk to you," I blurted out.

"Oh, Joshua, what's wrong now?" she asked.

I couldn't blame her for thinking the news was bad. Since we moved to Grandville, there had been plenty of it.

"It's okay, Mom," I reassured her. "The governor's coming to Grandville."

"To see you?" she asked. I could tell she was doubtful.

"I got a letter from him," I explained. "He wants to visit the toxic waste site."

"He actually wrote a letter to you?" She still couldn't believe it.

"I'll show it to you, Mom. And I got two more besides. One from Dad and one from McGee."

"My goodness, Joshua," she said. "Maybe I can leave a little early today. I can't wait until five o'clock

75

to see all this. See you in a little bit."

I had to tell somebody else my good news. Maybe Wendell was home.

He answered on the first ring.

"Wendell, you're not going to believe it," I said. "I got letters from the governor and McGee."

"Who are the Governor and McGee?" he asked. "Is that a new singing group?"

"Don't be a jerk, Wendell," I said. "The governor is the head of the state and McGee is in the videos."

"I don't get it," he said.

"C'mon over then," I said. "I'll show you."

Wendell was there in seconds, and I let him in the back door.

I spread out my mail on the kitchen table.

He picked up the envelope with the governor's seal embossed on it.

"Wow, this is impressive," he said. Then he looked at the letter.

"You've actually got his real signature," he said. "Not just some stamp. This could be worth a lot of money someday, especially if he ever gets to be president."

Leave it to Wendell to know all that political stuff.

"The governor and McGee, all in one day, " he went on. "I wonder who writes McGee's letters?"

"I don't know," I said. "I just sent it to the address Mr. Barron gave me."

"I hope I get to see the governor too," said Wendell.

"Of course," I said. "You'll go with me."

I heard my mom's car pull up.

"I've got to go," said Wendell. "I'm supposed to be cleaning my room."

"Hi, Wendell," Mom said as she breezed in the door. Then she turned toward me with a flourish of her hand. "And this must be Joshua McIntire, that well-known environmental activist from Grandville, Illinois."

"Aw, Mom," I said, "don't get silly."

"Your mom's right," said Wendell. "You're probably going to need a press secretary and an administrative assistant from now on."

"I don't even know what those are," I said.

"Don't hire anybody right away," said Wendell. "I can do both jobs."

My mom laughed. I wasn't sure I got the joke.

Wendell left and Mom gave me a high five and a hug.

"I am so proud of you, Joshua McIntire, that my buttons are about to burst," she said.

I just beamed.

"We'd better get some dinner on the table. You have karate tonight, and I'm going to church."

I looked at her in surprise. "What are you doing at church?"

77

"There's a women's group that meets on Wednesdays, and I thought I'd give it a try," she explained.

I smiled again. My face was all stretched out from smiling. It felt good for a change.

I couldn't wait to tell Mrs. Bannister. The minute I got to school I went right inside. The halls were deserted, and I remembered the time Ben and I had come in early with the cockroaches to hide in the teacher's desk. Wow, things had sure changed.

"Good morning, Joshua. What are you doing inside so early?" It was Mrs. Raymond, the principal, on her way toward the library. She looked a little worried.

"I've got something to tell Mrs. Bannister," I said.

"Does she know you're coming?" she asked.

"No," I said. "I just found this out last night."

"Let's go into the office and page her," she suggested.

Mrs. Bannister rounded the corner into the office just as her name boomed out over the intercom.

"Joshua, good morning. You're here bright and early," she greeted me.

"I couldn't wait to tell you, Mrs. Bannister. I invited the governor to Grandville, and he's coming."

Mrs. Bannister and Mrs. Raymond both let out shrieks. They were acting like teenagers.

"This is incredible, Joshua!" "Absolutely fantastic!" "You're marvelous!" "I don't believe it!" They took turns heaping praise on me.

I could listen to this all day, I thought.

"Are you absolutely certain?" asked Mrs. Bannister. She was coming back down to earth.

I pulled the letter out of my book bag.

She read it through quickly, then she gave another shriek. It was almost as good as the one she gave when we put cockroaches in her drawer. Fortunately this project wasn't going to get me in any trouble.

"We've got a lot of planning to do if the governor's coming to town," said Mrs. Raymond. "I'll have to call the mayor and the school superintendent."

Wait a minute, I thought. He's coming to see me, not the mayor and the school superintendent. But I decided to keep my mouth shut.

The morning flew by in a blur. I was enjoying my new found fame in 5B. But just before lunch, Mrs. Raymond's voice came over the intercom into the classroom.

"Mrs. Bannister, would you please send Joshua McIntire to the office?"

Secure in the knowledge that I wasn't in trouble, I hurried down the hall.

Mrs. Ellison, the social worker, was standing near the counter. She stuck out her hand. "Hi, Josh. I'm Mrs. Ellison."

79

I said hi.

"I understand you were asking about my services the other day," she said. "Would you like to chat for a few minutes?"

I wasn't sure what to do, but I nodded.

"Let's go down to my office."

I was embarrassed to be seen walking in the hall with her. What if someone saw me? They'd know I had problems. But she seemed to understand and hurried off to her office as if I weren't following.

"C'mon in," she invited. "I know it's hard for students to leave class to see the social worker. No one has to know if you don't want them to."

That made me feel better.

"Let me tell you about some of the things I do," she said. "Then we can decide if you'd like to come back and talk further.

"I see children who need someone to talk to about problems they're having. Sometimes kids have a hard time with a divorce in the family; maybe someone is sick or dies; or sometimes kids are just having a hard time making friends."

"Oh," I said.

"Do you think you'd like to talk about any of those things?" she asked.

"Well," I admitted, "my parents got divorced last year."

"I'll bet that was hard," she said.

"Yeah, it sure was."

"Do you keep hoping they might get back together again?" she asked.

I was surprised that she knew exactly what I was thinking.

"I've been praying for it every day," I blurted out without thinking. Then my face began to turn red.

"You don't need to be embarrassed, Josh," she assured me. "I pray too. But what are you going to do if God doesn't give you what you want?"

"But that's what God does," I replied.

"Oh, I know He answers our prayers," she said. "But sometimes He doesn't answer them in just the way we expect."

"I don't get it," I said.

"Let me give you an example," she went on. "Many years ago when my children were very young, I was feeling very discouraged and tired. I prayed for a vacation. The next week I went to the hospital with an emergency appendectomy. I thought God's answer should have been Florida."

I laughed. Then I thought quietly for a few seconds. I remembered a conversation I'd had with Mom. Something about asking God to help me feel better about everything and looking forward to the future.

Mrs. Ellison must have been reading my mind again.

"God doesn't always give us exactly what we

want, Josh," she explained. "But I do know that if we ask Him, He always helps us get through the hard times that happen in our lives."

I must have looked doubtful.

"He often sends other people to help us," she went on. "People who care about us and love us."

I knew right away who she was talking about— even though she couldn't have known. Sonny. Wendell. Mr. Barron. My mom. Trevor. Wow. Maybe God was answering my prayers after all.

"I'd be glad to be one of those people, Josh," she added. "We've got a group of kids who meet every week to talk about their feelings. All of their parents got divorced in the past year."

"No kidding," I said. "Here at Jefferson?"

"Sure, Joshua," she said. "You're not alone. Would you like to join the group?"

"I'm not sure. Could I think about it?"

"If you're not ready for the group, I'd be glad to talk with you individually for a while," she offered. "I also want you to know that I don't usually talk to students about God and prayer, Joshua. But since you talk to Him every day and I know Him too, it seemed like the right thing to do."

I didn't think things could possibly get any better. Dad, the governor, McGee, and now this.

I couldn't concentrate. If the governor's assistant didn't call Jefferson soon, I was going to explode. I had my report on toxic waste almost finished. I'd used eight different books in my research. When I read it to Aunt Kathy over the phone, she gave it an A+. I could hardly wait to show it to the governor.

I couldn't even keep my mind on a kickball game at recess. I left the game and sat on the steps to think. Ben Anderson followed me.

"Do you really think the governor's coming?" he asked.

"That's what my letter said," I replied.

"Boy, I sure wish I could meet the governor," he said.

Wendell came over and sat on the other side of me.

"Hi, Ben," Wendell said.

Ben hesitated before speaking. "Hi."

I was uneasy with Ben and Wendell there together.

They were so different.

"Ben, why don't you come to Awana with Josh and me next week?" Wendell asked out of the blue.

My heart sank. Why did Wendell have to get into that stuff now?

"Do you go, Josh?" he asked.

"Yeah," I said. I was embarrassed to admit it in front of Ben.

But he seemed to be interested. "Yeah," he said. "I'll go."

I couldn't believe it. Ben Anderson going to Awana! Wendell never ceased to amaze me. Ben Anderson was the last person in the world I would ever have invited to Awana.

But then I remembered my memory work for this week. "You are to go into all the world and preach the Good News to everyone, everywhere." Ben Anderson was the first person I should have invited to Awana. I just didn't have the nerve.

Mrs. Raymond was waiting for me just inside the door. "We got the call, Joshua. The governor is coming on Friday. They're faxing us his itinerary right away."

I knew what a fax machine was. Mom had one at her office. But what was an itinerary?

Mrs. Raymond was ready for everything. She'd planned an assembly in the gym. The chorus was going to sing the state song. We'd made banners on the computer. She'd ordered a Jefferson Jaguar sweatshirt for the governor. She even had the custodian washing and waxing the hallways. This visit was going to put Jefferson School on the map. She whirled through the school like a hurricane.

I, on the other hand, was paralyzed. Now that I knew he was coming and when, I began to worry. What would I wear? What would I say? What should I do? Did people bow to governors? Or was that just kings and queens? Would he shake my hand? The questions ran through my brain endlessly.

"What's your problem, Joshua?" Mom asked me at dinner. "You're going to meet the governor tomorrow and you're moping around here as though you just lost your best friend."

"I dunno," I said. "I guess I'm worried about what I'm going to say."

"Well, you wrote him such a terrific letter about the toxic waste site that you convinced him to come. Talk about that."

Mom was right. I knew all kinds of facts and figures about toxic waste. I'd practically been eating, breathing, and sleeping with toxic waste for the past two weeks. I'd tell him everything I knew. It was settled.

I'd found out what an itinerary was. It was a schedule of the places the governor would be going once he got to Grandville. He was landing in his airplane at the DuKane County Airport. First he was coming to Jefferson for the assembly. Then I was going to drive with him in his limousine over to the toxic waste site. The mayor was going to be there too. After that, the governor was holding a press conference at city hall.

Mom gave me my birthday present early, a new shirt and sweater. They looked great with the jeans I'd gotten for Christmas. I hoped the governor wouldn't think I was too dressed up.

The day was cold but sunny. Mom had taken a vacation day. "When my only child meets the governor, I'm going to be there no matter what," she said.

Sonny was closing his shop for the morning. Did that mean he and Mom would be together?

The governor arrived on schedule, and Mrs. Raymond and I met him at the school door. He looked a lot smaller than I expected, just like an ordinary person. He was wearing a blue suit and a red tie. He shook my hand and said he was happy to meet me, but there wasn't any time to talk. Mrs. Raymond just ushered him into the gym, and the kids started filing in. There were about six guys in gray suits and red ties hanging around the governor. Did he make them all dress the same?

Mrs. Raymond had forgotten to tell me what I

was supposed to be doing. My class wasn't in the gym yet. The Jefferson School band was beginning to play. Wendell played the clarinet and Tracy played the trumpet. I hoped they sounded better than at the Christmas concert.

My new sweater was beginning to itch. It was hot in the gym. Being an important person was hard work. I looked over toward the doorway and saw my mom and Sonny come in together. Did they just meet in the parking lot, or had they come together? I hadn't heard anything more about their going out, but whenever I thought about it, I still felt funny.

Mrs. Raymond's planning was perfect. Everything went off without a hitch. Now it was time for what I'd been waiting for since Wednesday—a ride in the governor's limousine. I'd never ridden in a limousine before.

Mrs. Raymond was winding up the assembly. "Students, parents, and friends. I want to say a special word of recognition for the student at Jefferson Elementary School who is responsible for Governor Henry being here today—Joshua McIntire. Joshua is a fifth grader in Mrs. Bannister's class, and he wrote to the governor and invited him."

The gym exploded in a cheer. Everyone was yelling and applauding me. I just felt hot. I didn't know whether it was embarrassment or my new sweater.

I tried to get Wendell's attention. I wanted him to meet the governor, but Ben was sticking to him like glue. I guessed I'd better introduce both of them.

I tried to remember whose name to say first in the introduction. Mom was always reminding me. "Governor Henry, I'd like you to meet my friends, Wendell Hathaway and Ben Anderson."

He shook each of their hands. "I'm delighted to know friends of Joshua's," he said. "I hope you boys have a good school year."

"Thank you," they answered together. Mrs. Bannister's class was lining up at the gym door and they joined the group. "See you later, Josh," they said.

The limousine was parked next to the custodian's pickup truck. It looked about twenty miles long. There was room inside for the governor, me, and all of the guys in gray suits.

"This is the part of the trip I've been waiting for, Joshua," said the governor. "I'm eager to hear your ideas about the toxic waste site and what you think we should do."

I couldn't believe that the governor actually wanted to talk to me. I was nervous in the beginning, but then I forgot who I was talking to and just told him the important facts from my report. He kept asking questions almost the whole way to the site.

"I think you should do something to make the

company that owned the factory move the poisonous chemicals out of town," I said. "Unless somebody important does something, they just won't listen."

"I think you're right, Joshua," the governor agreed.

One of the gray suit guys was writing everything down as we talked. He filled up six sheets of yellow paper. I suddenly realized that I hadn't even thought about my limo ride—I'd been too busy talking.

When we got to the site, the mayor was already there. We all put on hard hats and walked in through the eight-foot-high iron gate. The old red brick building and piles of rubble made it look like a bomb had fallen.

The grown-ups were talking now, but that was okay. I'd had my chance. A newspaper photographer was motioning to the mayor and me. He wanted a picture with the governor. I hoped it would turn out. I'd have something to send Dad.

As we came out through the gate, I wondered how I'd get back to school. Would the governor drop me off? Then I spied Mom and Sonny. They were strolling up the sidewalk talking to each other. What were they doing here?

"Hi, Josh," Mom called. Sonny called out a greeting too.

"We're here to take you to lunch," she said. "I talked to Mrs. Raymond, and she said it would be all right for you to miss some school."

"Your mom is taking a vacation day, and I've closed the shop. We've got some celebrating to do," Sonny said.

"Is this a date?" I asked.

"You can call it anything you want," Sonny answered. "I prefer to call it going to lunch with friends to celebrate Joshua McIntire's accomplishments. I've never known anyone who's ridden in the governor's limousine."

The three of us started toward the car. Mom tried to hold my hand, but I pulled away. I didn't want the governor to think I was a sissy. Sonny asked how it felt to ride in the limousine, and I told him all the details I could remember.

"Wanna sit in the front or the back?" he asked me as he unlocked the car door.

I remembered that Mom had always sat in the front seat when my dad drove.

"I'll sit in the back," I replied.

He helped my mom into the car.

As we drove toward The Sandpiper Restaurant, we talked nonstop. It reminded me of how things used to be when I was little. I felt like I was in a family again. Maybe I could persuade Sonny to take us both out on dates.